COUNTY PUBLIC LIBRARY

FRIENDS
OF ACPL

W9-BKU-238

STARRING ROSA

by
OTTO COONTZ

Little, Brown and Company

BOSTON   TORONTO

Also written and illustrated by Otto Coontz

The Quiet House

A Real Class Clown

COPYRIGHT © 1980 BY OTTO COONTZ

ALL RIGHTS RESERVED NO PART OF THIS BOOK MAY BE REPRODUCED IN ANY FORM
OR BY ANY ELECTRONIC OR MECHANICAL MEANS INCLUDING INFORMATION
STORAGE AND RETRIEVAL SYSTEMS WITHOUT PERMISSION IN WRITING FROM THE
PUBLISHER, EXCEPT BY A REVIEWER WHO MAY QUOTE BRIEF PASSAGES IN A REVIEW.

FIRST EDITION

Library of Congress Cataloging in Publication Data

Coontz, Otto.
  Starring Rosa.

  SUMMARY: A stagestruck pig's temporary job as a waitress leads to a starring role at Cook's Cafe.
  [1. Actors and actresses — Fiction. 2. Waiters and
waitresses — Fiction. 3. Pigs — Fiction] I. Title.
PZ7.C7845St   [E]   80-15925
ISBN 0-316-15535-7

Published simultaneously in Canada
by Little, Brown & Company (Canada) Limited

PRINTED IN THE UNITED STATES OF AMERICA

For John Keller, and for my sister, Clare

2111336

Rosa wanted to be on the stage more than anything. So she saved her money and moved to New York, where there were more stages than any other place in the world.

Rosa rented herself a room. Then she practiced her singing and her dancing and recited "Cinder-piglet" till she knew it by heart. Rosa decided to get a job as a chorus girl first thing in the morning.

But no one would let her audition. "We need a pig with experience," the talent scouts said. "Come back when you have some."

After a week, Rosa's money ran out. She had to take a job as a waitress at Cook's Café just to make ends meet. But Rosa had stars in her eyes. Even waiting tables, Rosa sang her heart out and danced from table to table. She hoped one day a big producer would come in and discover her.

The food at Cook's Café was not very good. But Rosa's service was worse. She couldn't balance a tray.

She always mixed up her orders.

Her uniforms startled the customers.

And she often added her checks wrong.

Her dancing jiggled the tables, and her singing hurt the cook's ears. Cook worried that Rosa's behavior would drive customers away. But nothing could stop her. When Rosa had a song in her heart, it just burst out of her.

Finally the cook could take no more. "Go!" he told her. "And don't come back!"

"Waiting tables took up too much time, anyway," Rosa said to herself. "Now I can spend all my time rehearsing."

The cook hired a new waitress. Her name was Anita. Her uniforms were dainty and starched, and she never dropped a tray.

Anita was quick and light on her feet. She never mixed up orders, and she always added right. Best of all, thought the cook, Anita *wanted* to be a waitress.

But business did not get better. In fact, each day it got worse. The service improved, but Cook's cooking didn't.

Without Rosa's entertainment, customers began to notice the food.

"Your cooking is awful!"

"You call this a meatball?"

"There's a clothespin in my pancake!"

2111336

Fewer people came to the diner. And anyone who did, came just to see Rosa.

"Is Rosa off today?"

"Did she go to Broadway?"

"Tell me when Rosa gets back!"

Cook got to thinking. That night he called Rosa.

"Rosa," said Cook, "maybe I made a mistake."

"No, Cook. You were right. I'd never make a good waitress."

"I agree," said Cook. "But I have an interesting idea. . . ."

The next day, Rosa went back to work. Part-time.

To help pay for her acting lessons.

For her first public appearance, Rosa was the tornado in *The Wizard of Oz.* She swept the audience off its feet.

Business was never better. In fact, customers waited in line to get in. And it wasn't for the food. Rosa was the hottest act in town.

In no time, Cook had to expand the café. Rosa's act was the talk of New York.

"What a tornado!"

"A voice like a nightingale!"

"That pig sure can dance!"